# Contents

# The Beavers' Christmas Tree

An extract from *Pilgrims of the Wild*
by Grey Owl

*Grey Owl is a naturalist, and Anahareo is his native
American wife. They are living in a log cabin and have
adopted two beavers, McGinnis and McGinty, as pets.*

*I* arrived home in the thick of the blizzard
and found the little cabin mighty snug
to come into out of the storm. Anahareo
had busied herself crocheting bright wool
borders on white sugar bags, split open and
freshly laundered, and we now had these for

# Making Angels in the Snow

## and other Christmas Stories

Miles Kelly

First published in 2015 by Miles Kelly Publishing Ltd
Harding's Barn, Bardfield End Green, Thaxted, Essex, CM6 3PX, UK

2 4 6 8 10 9 7 5 3

**Publishing Director** Belinda Gallagher
**Creative Director** Jo Cowan
**Editorial Director** Rosie Neave
**Senior Editor** Sarah Parkin
**Design Manager** Joe Jones
**Production** Elizabeth Collins, Caroline Kelly
**Reprographics** Stephan Davis, Jennifer Cozens, Thom Allaway
**Assets** Lorraine King

ISBN 978-1-78209-829-4

Printed in China

British Library Cataloguing-in-Publication Data
A catalogue record for this book is available from the British Library

ACKNOWLEDGEMENTS
The publishers would like to thank the following artists who have contributed to this book:

**Front cover:** Simona Sanfilippo (Plum Pudding Illustration Agency)

**Inside illustrations:**
**Decorative frame** Rachel Cloyne (Pickled Ink)
**The Beavers' Christmas Tree** Simona Sanfilippo (Plum Pudding Illustration Agency)
**Making Angels in the Snow** Natalia Moore (Advocate Art)
**The Wild Wood in Winter** Antonia Woodward (Plum Pudding Illustration Agency)
**Jimmy Scarecrow's Christmas** Charlotte Cooke (The Bright Agency)

Made with paper from a sustainable forest

www.mileskelly.net
info@mileskelly.net

window curtains, which gave everything a cosy, homey appearance.

Anahareo said the beavers had missed me. McGinnis especially had seemed to search for something, and had spent much time at the door, looking up at it. I offered them the sticks of candy I had for them, and which they sat and ate with loud and most unmannerly sounds of satisfaction.

I laid out my small purchases, which the kindly storekeeper had suggested that I make, saying as he did so that it must be lonesome in the woods and that he liked to feel that we had Christmas back there too. And being now in a country where Christmas was recognized as a real festival, we decided that we ought to make all the good cheer we could and so forget our troubles for a while.

I whittled out some boards of dry cedar, painted them with Indian designs, and attached them to the sides and tops of the windows where they looked, if not too closely inspected, like plaques of beadwork. We painted hanging ornaments with tribal emblems and hung them in places where the light fell on them. We laid two rugs of deerskin, which were immediately seized as play-toys by the two beavers, and had to be nailed down. We distributed coloured candles in prominent places, and hung a Japanese lantern from the rafter.

On Christmas Eve all was ready. But there was one thing missing. Anahareo decided that the beavers were to have a Christmas tree. So while I lit the lantern and arranged the candles, and put apples and oranges and nuts in dishes on the table, and tended the saddle of deer meat that sizzled alongside of the factory-made Christmas pudding that was boiling on top of the little stove, Anahareo went out into the starry Christmas night.

She was gone a little longer than I expected, and on looking out I saw her standing in rapt attention, listening. I asked her what she heard.

"Listen." She spoke softly. "Hear the Christmas bells," and pointed upwards.

I listened. A light breeze had sprung up and was flowing, humming in the pine tops far above. The breeze was whispering at first, then swelling louder in low undulating waves of sound, and sinking to a murmur, then ascending to a deep strong wavering note, fading again to a whisper. The pine trees – our Christmas bells.

Anahareo had got a fine balsam fir, which she wedged upright in a crevice in the floor poles. On top of it she put a lit candle, and on the limbs tied candies, pieces of apple and small delicacies from the table, so they hung by strings and could be reached.

Before long the beavers found the titbits and sampled them. Soon they were busy cutting the strings and pulling them down, and eating them with great gusto.

They soon consumed all there was on the tree, and as these were replaced, the little creatures stood up on their hind legs and grabbed and pulled at their presents. The beavers stole choice morsels from each other, pushing and shoving so that one would sometimes fall and scramble to his feet again as hastily as possible, for fear everything would be gone before he got up, while they screeched and chattered in their excitement.

We laughed and called out to them, and they would run to us excitedly and back to the tree with little noises as if to say, 'Just look what we found!' And when they could eat no more they started to carry away titbits, sometimes between their teeth, on all fours, or staggering along upright with some prized titbit clutched tightly in their arms, each apparently bent on getting all that could be got while it lasted.

And when we thought they had enough and no longer made replacements, McGinty pulled down the tree and started away with it, as though she figured on another crop appearing later and had decided to corner the source of supply.

It was the best fun of the evening, and instead of us making a festival for them, they made one for us, and provided us with a Christmas entertainment such as had never before been seen in any other home. And Anahareo was so happy to see her tree well appreciated, and the beavers were so happy to use it, and everybody seemed to be so thoroughly enjoying themselves, that I must be happy too just to see them so.

# Making Angels in the Snow

An extract from *Raggedy Andy Stories*
by Johnny Gruelle

"Whee! It's good to be back home again!" said Raggedy Andy to the other dolls, as he stretched his feet out in front of the little toy stove and rubbed his rag hands briskly together, as if to warm them through.

All the dolls laughed at Raggedy Andy for doing this, for they knew there had never been a fire in the little toy stove.

"We are so glad and happy to have you

back home again with us!" the dolls told Raggedy Andy.

"Well," Raggedy Andy replied, as he held his rag hands over the tiny lid of the stove and rubbed them again, "I have missed all of you and wished many times that you had been with me."

And as Raggedy Andy continued to hold his hands over the little stove, Uncle Clem asked him why he did it.

Raggedy Andy smiled and leaned back in his chair. "Really," he said, "I wasn't paying any attention. I've spent so much of my time while I was away drying out my soft cotton stuffing it seems as though it has almost become a habit."

"Were you wet most of the time, Raggedy Andy?" the French doll asked.

"Nearly all the time." Raggedy Andy

replied. "First I would get sopping wet and then I'd freeze!"

"Freeze!" exclaimed all the dolls together in one breath.

"Dear me, yes!" Raggedy Andy laughed. "Just see here." And he pulled his sleeve up and showed the dolls where his rag arm had been mended. "That was quite a rip!"

The dolls gathered around Raggedy Andy and examined the rip in his rag arm.

"It's all right now," he laughed. "But you should have seen me when it happened! I was frozen into one solid cake of ice all the way through, and when Marcella tried to limber up my arm before it had thawed out, it went *pop!* and just burst.

"Then I was placed in a pan of nice warm water until the icy cotton inside me had melted, and then I was hung up on a line above the kitchen stove, out at Gran'ma's."

"But how did you happen to get so wet and then freeze?" asked Raggedy Ann.

"Out across the road from Gran'ma's home, way out in the country, there is a lovely pond," Raggedy Andy explained. "When Marcella and I went out to Gran'ma's last week, Gran'ma met us with a sleigh, for the ground was covered with starry snow. The pretty pond was covered with ice, too, and upon the ice was a soft blanket of the white, white snow. It was so beautiful!" said Raggedy Andy.

"Gran'ma had a lovely new sled for Marcella, a red one with shiny runners.

"It was heaps of fun, for there was a little

hill at one end of the pond, so that when we coasted down, we went scooting across the pond like an arrow.

"Marcella would turn the sled sideways, just for fun, and she and I would fall off and go sliding across the ice upon our backs. Then Marcella showed me how to make angels in the soft snow!"

"Oh, tell us how, Raggedy Andy!" shouted all the dollies.

"It's very easy," said Raggedy Andy. "Marcella would lie down upon her back in the snow and put her hands back up over her head, then she would bring her hands in a circle down to her sides, like this." And Raggedy Andy lay upon the floor of the nursery and showed the dollies just how it was done. "Then," he added, "when she stood up it would leave the print of her

body and legs in the white, white snow, and
where she had swooped her arms there were
the angel's wings!"

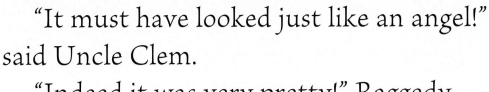

"It must have looked just like an angel!"
said Uncle Clem.

"Indeed it was very pretty!" Raggedy

Andy answered. "Then Marcella made a lot of angels by placing me in the snow and working my arms. So you see, what with falling off the sled so much and making so many angels, Marcella and I were both wet, but I was completely soaked through. My cotton just became soppy and I was ever so much heavier!

"Just as we were having a most delightful time, Gran'ma came to the door and 'Ooh-hooed' to Marcella to come and get a nice new doughnut. So Marcella, thinking to return in a minute, left me lying upon the sled and ran through the snow to Gran'ma's. And there I stayed until I began to feel stiff, and I could feel the cotton inside me begin to freeze.

"I lay upon the sled until after the sun went down. After it had been dark for some time, I heard someone coming through the snow and could see the yellow light of a lantern. It was Gran'ma.

"She pulled the sled over and then she picked me up and took me inside. 'He's frozen as stiff as a board!' she told Marcella as she handed me to her. Marcella did not say why she had forgotten to come for me, but I found out afterwards that it was because she was so wet. Gran'ma made her change her clothes and shoes, and would not permit her to go out and play again.

"Well, anyway," concluded Raggedy Andy. "That is the way it went all the time we were out at Gran'ma's – I was wet nearly all the time. But I wish you could all have been with me to share in the fun."

Raggedy Andy again leaned over the little toy stove and rubbed his rag hands

briskly together.
Uncle Clem went to the waste paper basket and came back with some scraps of yellow and red paper. Then, taking off one of the tiny lids, he stuffed the paper in part of the way, as if flames were shooting up!

Then, as all the dolls laughed, Raggedy Andy stopped rubbing his hands, caught Raggedy Ann about the waist, and went skipping across the nursery floor with her.

# The Wild Wood in Winter

Adapted from *The Wind in the Willows*
by Kenneth Grahame

*Mole and Rat live together. Mole has often wanted
to meet Mr Badger, but Badger lives in the Wild Wood
and Rat has told Mole never to go there.*

There was plenty to talk about on those short winter days when the animals found themselves round the fire. Still, the Mole had a good deal of spare time, and one afternoon he decided to go and explore the Wild Wood, and perhaps meet Mr Badger.

It was a cold, still afternoon when the Mole slipped out of the warm parlour into the open air, and pushed on towards the Wild Wood. There was nothing to alarm him at first entry. Twigs crackled under his feet, logs tripped him, but that was all fun and exciting.

Then the faces began.

It was over his shoulder, that he first thought he saw a face, a little, evil face, looking out at him from a hole. When he turned, the thing had vanished.

The Mole passed another hole, and another, and another. And then – yes! – no! – yes! Certainly a little, narrow face, with hard eyes, had flashed up for an instant, and was gone. If he could only get away from the holes in the banks, he thought, there would be no more faces. He swung off the path and plunged into the untrodden places of the wood.

Then the whistling began.

Very faint and shrill it was, and far behind him, but somehow it made him hurry forwards. Then, still very faint and shrill, it sounded far ahead of him, and made him hesitate and want to go back. As the Mole stood still, a rabbit came running hard towards him. He waited, expecting it to swerve from him. Instead, the animal almost brushed him as it dashed past.

"Get out of this, you fool, get out!" the Mole heard him mutter as he disappeared down a friendly burrow.

In panic, the Mole began to run too. He ran up against things, he fell over things and into things. At last he took refuge in the deep, dark hollow of an old beech tree.

He was too tired to run, and could only snuggle down into the dry leaves and hope he was now safe for a time.

Meantime the Rat, warm and comfortable, dozed by his fireside. Then the fire crackled and he woke with a start. He reached down to the floor for his verses, and then looked round for the Mole.

But the Mole was not there.

The Rat left the house and carefully examined the ground outside, hoping to find the Mole's tracks. There they were, sure enough, leading directly into the Wild

Wood. The Rat re-entered the house, strapped a belt round his waist, shoved a brace of pistols into it and set off for the Wild Wood.

It was already getting towards dusk when he plunged into the wood, all the time calling out cheerfully, "Moly! Where are you? It's me – it's old Rat!"

He had patiently hunted through the wood for an hour or more, when at last he heard a little answering cry. He made his way to the foot of an old beech tree, with a hole in it, and from out of the hole came a voice, saying, "Ratty! Is that really you?"

The Rat crept into the hollow, and there, sure enough, he found the Mole, exhausted and still trembling.

"Oh Rat!" the Mole cried, "I've been so terribly frightened!"

"I quite understand," said the Rat soothingly. "You shouldn't really have gone and done it, Mole."

The Mole was greatly cheered by the sight of the Rat and he stopped shivering.

"Now then," said the Rat, "we really must make a start for home. It will never do to spend the night here. It is far too cold, for one thing."

"Dear Ratty," said the Mole. "I'm sorry, but you must let me rest here a while longer, if I'm to get home at all."

"Oh, all right," said the Rat, "rest away."

So the Mole got well into the dry leaves and presently dropped off into sleep, while the Rat covered himself up, too, and lay patiently waiting.

When at last the Mole woke up, the Rat said, "Now then! We really must be off."

He put his head out. Then the Mole heard him saying quietly to himself, "Hello."

"What's up, Ratty?" asked the Mole.

"Snow is up," replied the Rat briefly, "or rather, down. It's snowing hard. Still, we must make a start. The worst of it is, I don't exactly know where we are."

An hour or two later – they had lost all count of time – they pulled up. The snow was getting so deep that they could hardly drag their little legs through it. There seemed to be no end to this wood and, worst of all, no way out.

"We can't sit here very long," said the Rat. "There's a sort of dell down here where the ground seems all hilly and hummocky. We'll make our way into that, and try and find some sort of shelter."

They were investigating one of the

hummocky bits when the point of the Rat's stick struck something that sounded hollow. He worked till he could get a paw through, and then called the Mole to come and help him. At last the result of their labours stood full in view.

In the side of what had seemed to be a snowbank stood a solid-looking little door. On a small brass plate, they could read by the aid of moonlight: MR BADGER. The Mole fell backwards on the snow from sheer surprise and delight. "Rat!" he cried, "you're a wonder!" He sprang up at the bell pull, clutched it and swung there, and from quite a long way off they could faintly hear a deep-toned bell.

There was the noise of a bolt shot back, and the door opened a few inches, enough to show a long snout and a pair of sleepy blinking eyes.

"Now, the very next time this happens," said a gruff and suspicious voice, "I shall be exceedingly angry. Who is it this time, disturbing people on a night like this? Speak up now!"

"Oh, Badger," cried the Rat, "let us in, please. It's me, Rat, and my friend Mole, and we've lost our way in the snow."

"What, Ratty, my dear little man!" exclaimed the Badger, in quite a different voice. "Come along in, both of you, at once. Well, I never! Lost in the snow!"

The two animals heard the door shut behind them with great joy and relief.

The Badger looked kindly down on them. "This is not the sort of night for small animals to be out," he said. "Come into the kitchen. There's a first-rate fire there, and supper and everything."

He shuffled on in front of them, carrying the light, and they followed him, down a long, gloomy passage, into all the glow and warmth of a large fire-lit kitchen. The floor was well-worn red brick, and on the wide hearth burned a fire of logs.

The kindly Badger thrust them down on a settle to toast

themselves at the fire, and he bade them remove their wet coats and boots. Then he fetched them dressing gowns and slippers.

In the embracing light and warmth, warm and dry at last, with weary legs propped up in front of them, and a clink of plates being arranged on the table, it seemed to the storm-driven animals that the cold and trackless Wild Wood, just left outside, was miles and miles away, and all that they had suffered in it a half-forgotten dream.

# Jimmy Scarecrow's Christmas

By Mary E Wilkins Freeman

Jimmy Scarecrow led a sad life in the winter. He liked to be useful, and in winter he was absolutely of no use at all.

On Christmas Eve, Santa Claus came in his sledge. He was on his way to the farmhouse where Betsey lived with her Aunt Hannah. Santa Claus had a doll baby for her, and when poor Jimmy Scarecrow saw him, his heart gave a great leap.

"Santa Claus, please give me a little present. I was good all summer and kept the crows out of the corn," pleaded the poor scarecrow, but Santa Claus passed by.

The next morning, Betsey sat at the window holding her doll baby, and she looked out at Jimmy Scarecrow standing alone in the field amidst the corn stubble.

"Aunt Hannah, did Santa Claus bring the scarecrow a Christmas present?" she said.

"No, of course he didn't." Aunt Hannah replied. She was making a patchwork quilt.

"Why not?"

"Because he's a scarecrow. Don't ask such silly questions."

"I wouldn't like to be treated so, if I was a scarecrow," said Betsey.

It was snowing hard out of doors. The scarecrow's poor old coat got whiter and whiter. Aunt Hannah worked until the middle of the afternoon on her quilt. Then she got up and spread it out over the sofa with an air of pride.

"There," she said, "that's done. I've got one for every bed in the house, and I've given four away. I'd give this away if I knew of anybody that wanted it."

Aunt Hannah put on her shawl and set out to visit her sister, who lived down the road. Half an hour after Aunt Hannah had gone, Betsey put her little red shawl over her head, and ran across the field to Jimmy Scarecrow. She carried her new doll baby snuggled up under her shawl.

"Merry Christmas!" she said.

"Wish you the same," said Jimmy.

Betsey looked at the old hat fringed with icicles, and the old snow-laden coat.

"I've brought you a Christmas present," she said, and with that she tucked her doll baby inside Jimmy Scarecrow's old coat.

"Thank you," said Jimmy Scarecrow.

"You're welcome," she said. "Keep her under your coat, so the snow won't wet her."

"Yes, I will," said Jimmy Scarecrow.

"Don't you feel cold in that old summer coat?"

"If I had a little exercise, I should be warm," he replied. But he shivered, and the wind whistled through his rags.

"Wait a minute,"

said Betsey, then she was off across the field.

Jimmy Scarecrow stood in the corn stubble, and soon Betsey was back again with Aunt Hannah's quilt.

"Here," she said, "here is something to keep you warm," and she folded the quilt around the scarecrow.

"Aunt Hannah wants to give it away if anybody wants it," she said. "Goodbye." Then she ran across the field, and left Jimmy Scarecrow alone with the quilt and doll baby.

Jimmy Scarecrow had never felt so happy in his life as he did for an hour or so. But after that the snow began to turn to rain, and the quilt was soaked through. So was his coat and the poor doll baby.

Suddenly he again heard Santa Claus' sleigh bells.

"Santa Claus!" cried Jimmy Scarecrow, and this time Santa Claus heard him.

"Who's there?" Santa Claus shouted out of the darkness.

"Jimmy Scarecrow!"

"Have you been standing here ever since corn was ripe?" Santa Claus asked pityingly, and Jimmy replied that he had.

"What's that over your shoulders?" Santa Claus continued.

"It's a quilt."

"And what's that you're holding under your coat?"

"The doll baby that Betsey gave to me, and I'm afraid it's dead," poor Jimmy Scarecrow sobbed.

"Nonsense!" cried Santa Claus. "Let me

see it!" And with that he pulled the doll baby out from under the scarecrow's coat, patted its back, and it began to cry.

"It's all right," said Santa Claus. "Now get into the sledge, Jimmy Scarecrow, and come with me to the North Pole!" he cried.

"Please, how long shall I stay?" asked Jimmy Scarecrow.

"Why, you are going to live with me," replied Santa Claus. "I've been looking for a person like you for a long time."

"Are there any crows to scare away at the North Pole?" Jimmy Scarecrow asked.

"No," answered Santa Claus, "I want you to scare away Arctic explorers from the North Pole. Come along – I am in a hurry."

"I will go on two conditions," said Jimmy. "First, I want to make a present for Aunt Hannah and Betsey, next Christmas."

"You shall make them any present you choose. What else?"

"I want some way provided to scare the crows out of the corn next summer."

"That is easily managed," said Santa Claus. "Just wait a minute."

Santa Claus went with his lantern close to one of the fence posts and wrote a notice to the crows upon it in crow language.

"The corn will be safe now," he said.

Then Jimmy got into the sledge and they flew away over the fields.

The next morning there was much surprise at the farmhouse, when Aunt Hannah and Betsey looked out of the window and the scarecrow was gone, and the quilt and the doll baby with him.

"We'll have to have another scarecrow next summer," said Aunt Hannah.

But the next summer there was no need of a scarecrow, for not a single grain was stolen by a crow.

"It is a great mystery to me why the crows don't come into our cornfield," said Aunt Hannah.

But she had a still greater mystery to solve when Christmas came round again. She and Betsey each found a strange present on Christmas morning. Aunt Hannah's present was her old quilt, remodelled, and Betsey's present was her doll baby of the Christmas before, but it was a year older.

Neither Aunt Hannah nor Betsey knew that the quilt and the doll were Jimmy Scarecrow's Christmas presents to them.